John Burningham

COURTNEY

CROWN PUBLISHERS, INC.

New York

Copyright © 1994 by John Burningham

Published by Crown Publishers, Inc., a Random House company,
201 East 50th Street, New York, New York 10022. Originally published in the United Kingdom
by Jonathan Cape Ltd. in 1994.

CROWN is a trademark of Crown Publishers, Inc.

Manufactured in Singapore

Library of Congress Cataloging-in-Publication Data
Burningham, John.
Courtney / by John Burningham.
p. cm.
"Originally published in the United Kingdom by Jonathan Cape Ltd. in 1994"–T.p. verso.
Summary: The children bring home an old mongrel named Courtney who cooks, serves
meals, juggles, and even saves the baby from a fire, only to disappear mysteriously.
[1. Dogs—Fiction. 2. Family life—Fiction.] I. Title.
PZ7.B936Cp   1994
[E]—dc20   93-43508

ISBN 0-517-59883-3 (trade)
0-517-59884-1 (lib. bdg.)

10 9 8 7 6 5 4 3 2 1

"We would really like to have a dog," the children said. "Our house would be much better with a dog. The dog would guard the house and it could play with us."

"There are lots of lovely dogs at the Dogs' Home. Can't we please have one?"

"Dogs need feeding and walking."

"And they make a mess everywhere."

"We will walk the dog and feed it."

"And we will clean up the mess."

"Please, can we?"

"Oh, very well then, if you must."

"Make sure it's a proper dog. One with a pedigree."
"And remember, you'll both have to take care of it."

The children looked at lots of dogs. None of them seemed to
be what they wanted.

"Have you a dog that nobody wants?" they asked the man. "All the dogs we have seen will find homes easily."

"We do have a dog called Courtney," said the man. "Nobody wants Courtney."

"We don't know anything about him," said the man. "We don't know where he came from. Nobody wants him and he's an old dog."
"We want Courtney," said the children, and they took him home.

"What on earth have you got there?" said the parents. "Why didn't you get a proper dog? He's old and he's a mongrel, not a pedigree like we said."
"But Courtney's lovely," said the children.

"Well, it's getting late now and you must be going to bed. Courtney will have to sleep in the kitchen."

The next morning, the children raced down to the kitchen to see their new dog, but Courtney was not there.

"We said the dog was no good. These mongrels, you can't rely on them. Why on earth didn't you get a proper dog like we said?"

That afternoon, Courtney came back, dragging a large trunk
behind him.

Once in the house, he opened the trunk, put on a chef's hat and apron, and immediately began to cook a delicious meal.

He changed into waiter's clothes and served the family round the table.

Courtney then played the violin while the family finished the meal.

Out of his trunk, he took some things to juggle with and
entertain the baby.

Sometimes Courtney would meet other dogs in the park.

But most of the time he spent with the family.

One day, the house caught fire, and the family was outside waiting for the fire engines to arrive.

"Where's Courtney?" said one of the children.
"Where's my baby?" shrieked the mother.

Then they saw Courtney climbing down the ladder, holding the baby.

The fire was put out and the house soon repaired, and the
family was able to carry on living as usual.

One morning they came downstairs and Courtney was not there. The children looked everywhere, but they could not find Courtney or his trunk. "We told you the dog was no good," said the parents. "If they are not thoroughbreds, you cannot rely on them."

The children went to the police station. "We've lost our dog. He's quite old, with big eyebrows. He can play the violin, cook wonderful dinners, and he juggles to entertain the baby."

"I'll certainly let you know if an old dog with big eyebrows who can play the violin, cook wonderful dinners, and juggle to keep the baby amused is brought in," said the policeman.

That summer, the family went on vacation to the seashore and they took a boat with them.

Every day the children went out in the boat. The boat was always tied to a rock with a long piece of rope so it would not drift out to sea. But on the last day something awful happened . . .

The rope broke.

They lost the oars.

The boat drifted out to sea.

"Somebody help us!" cried the mother.

The boat had drifted almost out of sight.

Then suddenly there was a tug.

The boat was being pulled by something.   Toward the shore.

They never did find out who or what it was that had pulled
their boat back to shore.

I wonder what it could have been.